Milly-Molly-Mandy

and Billy Blunt

D1637762

Books about Milly-Molly-Mandy from
Macmillan Children's Books

Milly-Molly-Mandy Stories

More of Milly-Molly-Mandy

Further Doings of Milly-Molly-Mandy

Milly-Molly-Mandy Again

Milly-Molly-Mandy & Co

Milly-Molly-Mandy and Billy Blunt

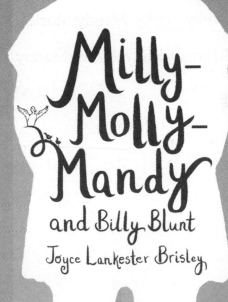

Milly-Molly-Mandy
and Billy Blunt

Joyce Lankester Brisley

MACMILLAN CHILDREN'S BOOKS

First published by George G. Harrap 1967

This edition published 2019 by Macmillan Children's Books
an imprint of Pan Macmillan
20 New Wharf Road, London N1 9RR
Associated companies throughout the world
www.panmacmillan.com

ISBN 978-1-5290-1067-1

3 5 7 9 8 6 4 2

A CIP catalogue record for this book is available from
the British Library.

Typeset by The Dimpse
Printed and bound by CPI Group (UK) Ltd, Croydon CR0 4YY

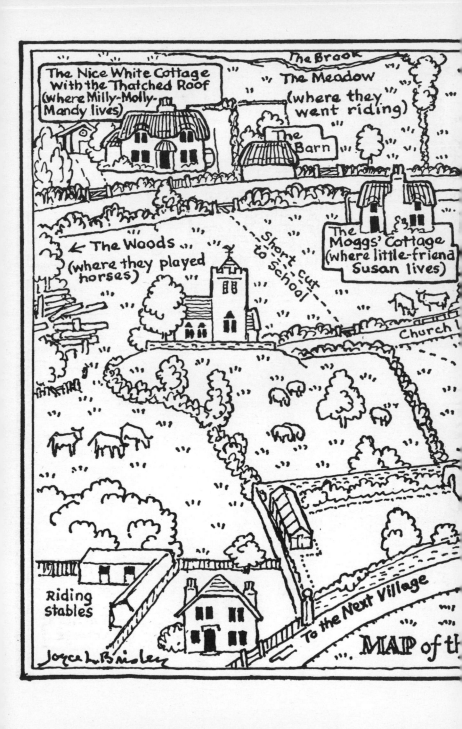

Contents

1

Milly-Molly-Mandy Rides a Horse

Once upon a time Milly-Molly-Mandy was out playing at horses with little-friend-Susan and Billy Blunt.

There was a clearing in the woods near the nice white cottage with the thatched

roof, where Milly-Molly-Mandy lived, and they had found some fallen branches and were galloping astride them along a mossy track.

Then Billy Blunt saw a low-growing branch of a tree which he climbed on, and sat bouncing up and down exactly like real horse-riding. Milly-Molly-Mandy and little-friend-Susan had to stop and watch him, till he let them each have a go.

Then he said firmly, "Now it's my turn." And he got on again and bounced solemnly up and down, while Milly-Molly-Mandy and little-friend-Susan pranced around on their sticks.

(Horse-riding is very good exercise!)

Presently what did they hear but a thud-

thudding sound, like real horses' hoofs. And what did they see but five or six real horse-riders come riding along down the mossy track.

"Oh, look!" cried Milly-Molly-Mandy.

"Live horses!" cried little-friend-Susan.

"Mind yourselves!" called Billy Blunt, from his tree.

So they stood well to one side as the horses passed in single file, hoofs thudding, harnesses creaking, breaths snorting.

Milly-Molly-Mandy and little-friend-Susan and Billy Blunt hardly looked at the riders, till one small one in fawn knee-breeches turned her head and said, "Hullo!" to them.

It was the little girl Jessamine, who lived

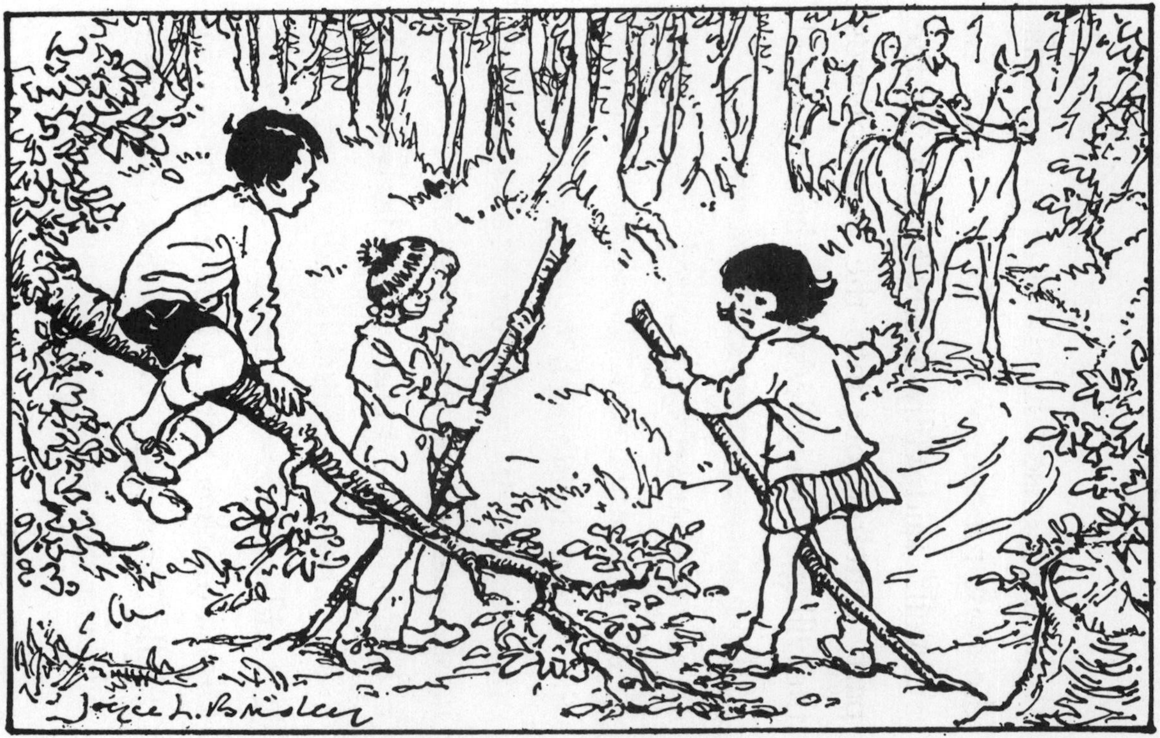

"Oh, look!" cried Milly-Molly-Mandy

at the Big House with the iron railings near the cross-roads.

"Well!" said Milly-Molly-Mandy, as the party cantered out into the road towards the village; "fancy Jessamine having a real horse!"

"Isn't she lucky!" said little-friend-Susan.

"It's the riding school," said Billy Blunt. "She's learning riding."

Somehow, their pretend-horses didn't seem quite such fun now. Billy Blunt stopped bouncing and climbed down.

"I wish we'd got real horses to ride on," said Milly-Molly-Mandy.

"So do I," said little-friend-Susan.

Billy Blunt said, "Well, what about your old Twinkletoes?"

"He's Grandpa's pony," said Milly-Molly-Mandy. "He isn't meant for riding."

"He pulls their market-cart," said little-friend-Susan.

"But he is a horse," said Billy Blunt.

Milly-Molly-Mandy stood and thought.

"I don't believe they'd let us ride him," she said; "but we could *ask*, couldn't we?"

"Oh, *do!*" said little-friend-Susan.

"No harm asking," said Billy Blunt.

So they all ran down the road to the nice white cottage with the thatched roof, into the kitchen, where Mother was busy ironing shirts.

"Oh, Mother!" asked Milly-Molly-Mandy. "Please may we go horse-riding on Twinkletoes?"

"Well, now!" said Mother; "you'd better see what Father has to say!"

So they ran outside to the barn, where Father was busy sorting potatoes.

"Father!" asked Milly-Molly-Mandy. "Please may we go horse-riding on Twinkletoes?"

"Why, where do you want to go?" asked Father. "Land's End or John o'Groats?"

"Oh, no," said Milly-Molly-Mandy (she wasn't sure where either of those places were), "only just in the meadow, perhaps—"

"Well, now," said Father, "perhaps you'd better see what Grandpa has to say!"

So they ran around to the stable, where Grandpa was busy mending a broken strap.

"Grandpa!" asked Milly-Molly-Mandy;

"please may we go horse-riding on Twinkletoes?"

Grandpa didn't answer at once. Then he said slowly:

"Well, you know, he's not exactly used to folks sitting on him, is old Twinkletoes. But we might try!"

So Grandpa tried putting a bridle on Twinkletoes and strapping an old blanket across his back for a saddle. Then he stooped to lift Milly-Molly-Mandy up.

But Milly-Molly-Mandy said quickly, "Billy Blunt ought to have first go!" (Maybe she wanted to see if Twinkletoes would mind being ridden!)

So Grandpa held the bridle while Billy Blunt got on. And after a moment

Twinkletoes clip-clopped slowly across the yard, with Billy Blunt sitting joggling on his back.

They all went into the meadow, and Grandpa stood by the gate, watching. It was very exciting!

"Does it feel nice?" Milly-Molly-Mandy called up to Billy Blunt.

"It looks lovely!" called little-friend-Susan.

"Not bad," returned Billy Blunt. (He was really enjoying it like anything!) "Look out you don't get under his feet!"

They went right across the meadow, and Twinkletoes didn't seem to mind a bit. When they got back to the gate again Billy Blunt slid down, and then Grandpa helped little-friend-Susan up. (Milly-Molly-Mandy had to keep jumping because it was so exciting and so hard to wait her turn! – but of course visitors should have first go.)

Little-friend-Susan only wished that old Twinkletoes wouldn't keep stopping to nibble the grass!

At last Milly-Molly-Mandy's turn came.

She was lifted on to the pony's broad back (it felt awfully high!) and off he went, with Milly-Molly-Mandy holding tight to his mane.

It was terribly thrilling! But soon she was able to sit up and look about a bit. It felt rather like being on a rocking-chair, as Twinkletoes ambled slowly along with his head drooping, while little-friend-Susan picked daisies and Billy Blunt romped with Toby the dog.

Suddenly – what *do* you think? – Twinkletoes seemed to stumble on a rough bit of ground. And next moment Milly-Molly-Mandy slid sprawling over his head down into the long grass!

The others all came running to help her up, Toby the dog barking at poor Twinkletoes, who stood shaking his head in a puzzled sort of way.

"You let his head hang down, didn't you?" said Grandpa; "and he kind of went to sleep! You want to let him feel the reins, only don't pull on them. You'll learn. Up with you, now!"

But Milly-Molly-Mandy wasn't sure she wanted any more riding just at present. "It's Billy's turn again," she said.

But Billy Blunt said, "No! You should always get on at once if you fall off a horse. Go on, get on."

So then Milly-Molly-Mandy got on. And Twinkletoes trotted with her so nicely round the meadow that they all forgot about the tumble.

"Can we have some more rides soon?"

asked Milly-Molly-Mandy, as she got down and they all stood patting Twinkletoes.

Grandpa said, yes, another day, when he had had time to see about some stirrups.

Milly-Molly-Mandy and Billy Blunt and little-friend-Susan were glad to think they had a real horse to ride on now, like the little girl Jessamine!

2

Milly-Molly-Mandy
Does an Errand

Once upon a time Milly-Molly-Mandy went on an errand to the village. (It was only to get a tin of cocoa which Mother had forgotten to order.)

When she came to the grocer's shop Mr Smale the grocer was outside his door, opening up a box of kippers. (Kippers do smell rather kippery, so Milly-

Molly-Mandy guessed Mr Smale preferred to keep them outside – where people passing could see them too: he didn't often sell kippers.)

While Milly-Molly-Mandy waited till he had done, someone came out of the baker's shop next door, carrying a heavy shopping-basket and an umbrella, as well as a loaf of bread.

It was one of the Miss Thumbles, who lived in a cottage by the duck-pond. There were two Miss Thumbles, sisters, both so alike that the only way Milly-Molly-Mandy could tell them apart was that one always seemed to wear a hat, even to go in the garden. That was Miss Thumble. The other one, of course, was the Other Miss Thumble.

But today, being rather cold and windy, this Miss Thumble wore a warm woolly scarf tied over her grey hair. So Milly-Molly-Mandy really couldn't be sure whether she were Miss Thumble or the Other Miss Thumble.

Seeing the newly opened box of kippers, Miss Thumble (or perhaps it was the Other Miss Thumble) stopped and said:

"Dear me! I should like a couple of those – my sister does enjoy a nice grilled kipper for her tea! But how I'm going to manage to carry everything—"

Mr Smale quickly clapped two flat glistening brown kippers together and went into the shop to wrap them up. So Milly-Molly-Mandy said:

"Shall I carry your bread for you?"

And she took it, while Miss Thumble thankfully put her basket down on the step to find her purse, and went inside to pay.

As Milly-Molly-Mandy waited there, with the loaf of bread and the basket, who should look over the Blunts' garden gate opposite but Billy Blunt! He came out and strolled across the road, hands in pockets.

"Hullo! That's not your basket," said Billy Blunt.

"No," said Milly-Molly-Mandy. "It's Miss Thumble's. I'm helping to carry her things."

"You can't carry that," said Billy Blunt.

"Yes, I can," said Milly-Molly-Mandy. "Some of it."

"It's too heavy," said Billy Blunt.

Milly-Molly-Mandy rather hoped he was going to offer to help too. But he only turned and went back in at the garden gate, just as Miss Thumble came out of the shop.

She thanked Milly-Molly-Mandy for keeping an eye on her basket, and tried to find room in it for the parcel of kippers. But one thing and another kept falling out – potatoes and cheese and a big round cabbage – rolling about on the pavement.

Milly-Molly-Mandy picked them up, very nearly dropping the loaf at the same time.

"Here, give 'em here," said Billy Blunt.

He had come out again, pulling his little

old box-on-wheels with him.

Putting the heavy basket into it, with all the odd potatoes and kippers and things, he set off hauling it along the road, past the forge and round by the duck-pond, Milly-Molly-Mandy following hugging the loaf, and Miss Thumble stumping after them

looking as pleased as anything!

By the little cottages they stopped, and Miss Thumble rattled the letter-box of one. And presently the door opened; and there was the other Miss Thumble, wearing felt slippers *and* a hat. (So Milly-Molly-Mandy knew *she* must be Miss Thumble, and the first one was the Other Miss Thumble.)

They all helped to pile the things on to the kitchen table, and both the Miss Thumbles were very grateful at having so much kind help.

"I know my sister finds the shopping very heavy at times," said Miss Thumble.

"But I don't usually have quite so much to carry all at once!" said the Other Miss Thumble.

She opened one of the packages for her sister to offer the visitors each a biscuit before they left. And though Billy Blunt wasn't too keen on oatmeal biscuits he took one and said thank-you nicely, and so did Milly-Molly-Mandy. (She liked all kinds of biscuits – but some more than others, of course!)

They walked, munching together, back with the empty cart as far as the Blunts' gate.

Billy Blunt said, "We'd better see if they'd like us to carry their shopping for them other times."

"Yes, let's!" said Milly-Molly-Mandy. "They haven't anyone to run errands for them."

And then she suddenly remembered her own errand!

And she said goodbye to Billy Blunt and ran across the road to the grocer's to get the tin of cocoa for Mother. (The kippers, she noticed, were nearly sold out already.)

When she got home to the nice white cottage with the thatched roof she told Mother all about the Miss Thumbles, and also about the kippers at the grocer's. Mother said:

"Yes! Father happened to be passing, and he saw them too. He's just bought a dozen."

So that evening, when Father and Mother and Grandpa and Grandma and Uncle and Aunty sat down to enjoy their kippers (Milly-Molly-Mandy had half a one, with the bones carefully picked out,

SAT DOWN TO ENJOY THEIR KIPPERS

on a slice of
toast) they liked
to think of Miss
Thumble and the
Other Miss Thumble
enjoying their kippers too!

3

Milly-Molly-Mandy
Finds a Parcel

Once upon a time Milly-Molly-Mandy
walked down to the village with little-
friend-Susan, who had to buy some things

for her mother
at Mr Smale
the grocer's
shop. (It's
always nicer
to do that sort
of thing with
somebody than
just by yourself.)

While she waited outside (because there were several people in the shop, so it was rather full) Milly-Molly-Mandy noticed a man, coming along the pavement opposite, stoop as if to pick up something. Then he straightened himself, looked around, and said "Ha Ha!" rather loudly, and walked on.

Milly-Molly-Mandy thought it seemed a bit funny; but grown-ups sometimes did do funny things, so she didn't think more about it. And little-friend-Susan came out just then with a big bag in her arms.

"Let's have a look in Miss Muggins' shop!" said Milly-Molly-Mandy.

So they crossed over and looked in the window (because Miss Muggins sold toys and sweets as well as ladies' things, and it's always fun to see what you might buy if you could!).

But there was nothing new, so they were just going on when Milly-Molly-Mandy said:

"Look! What's this?"

"What's what?" said little-friend-Susan, clutching her bag.

Milly-Molly-Mandy pointed.

"Someone must have dropped it," she said.

It was a neat little parcel tied with string.

Milly-Molly-Mandy bent to pick it up. But – what *do* you think? – it slid away from her along the pavement! She let out a squeal, and little-friend-Susan dropped an orange from her bag.

"SOMEONE MUST HAVE DROPPED IT," SHE SAID

But, while picking it up for her, Milly-Molly-Mandy noticed something! Pushing the orange back in the bag, she whispered:

"Susan! don't talk loud, but there's some black cotton tied to that parcel, and I think it goes behind the fence into the Blunts' garden!" Then in her usual voice she said, "We'd best hurry home before you drop any more things, Susan!" – as if quite forgetting what was on the ground.

Then she crept to the fence adjoining Miss Muggins' shop and peeped over. And behind some bushes in the Blunts' garden she could just see a bit of Billy Blunt's leg!

"Ha ha!" she called out (like the man she had watched), "we can see you! You thought you'd had us, didn't you?"

Billy Blunt's grinning face looked round the bush. "So I did," he said, "had you nicely!"

"Can we come in there with you, and watch?" said little-friend-Susan. "There's someone coming along!"

"Hurry up, then, and don't make a lot of row," said Billy Blunt.

So Milly-Molly-Mandy and little-friend-  Susan hurried in at the gate and over to the bushes where Billy Blunt was hiding. And they made themselves as small as possible behind him, while he held the end of his thread and waited.

Young Mrs Rudge the blacksmith's wife, going to see if Miss Muggins sold hair-curlers (she did), stooped to pick up the package. Billy Blunt twitched it away from her, and she called out, "Now, Billy Blunt! – you and your monkey-tricks!" – though she couldn't have seen him!

Then Miss Muggins' Jilly came by with a handful of chocolate-drops (which her aunty must have given her). She nearly trod on the little parcel before she saw it.

Billy Blunt pulled the thread, but Miss Muggins' Jilly's foot was on it, and the cotton broke.

She picked up the package (not noticing the bit of black thread dangling), and, seeing the stamp, supposed it had been dropped by somebody going to the post. So, like a thoughtful little girl, she went and popped it into the letter-box outside Mr Smale the grocer's shop!

"Ohhh!" whispered Milly-Molly-Mandy and little-friend-Susan together, watching from the other side of the fence. "She's posted it!"

Billy Blunt doubled up with silent laughter.

"She never noticed the address – and that it wasn't a proper stamp!"

"What had you put on it?" whispered Milly-Molly-Mandy.

"Mr Nobody, Grand View, The Moon –

and a stamp off an old envelope!"

They all nearly burst with laughing, in among the bushes.

"But the postman can't deliver it, so what will he do?" whispered little-friend-Susan.

"He'll have to open it!" Billy Blunt exploded.

"What's inside?" they asked.

"Ssh! – just a stone and a bit of paper with 'Ever been had?'" Billy Blunt said, and set them all off again.

"Oh, but poor Mr Jakes," said Milly-Molly-Mandy, then, "and he's such a nice postman! It's too bad to take him in!"

"But I never meant for him to be taken in," said Billy Blunt, "and he mustn't ever know who's done it."

"Can't we do something nice to make up?" said Milly-Molly-Mandy.

"Send him something nice in a parcel," said little-friend-Susan.

"Then he might suspect," said Billy Blunt; "and after all, *we* didn't post it!"

Miss Muggins' Jilly had gone now, so they could come out of hiding and laugh all they wanted, as they couldn't fool anyone else now. Little-friend-Susan took up her shopping-bag.

But then Milly-Molly-Mandy had a bright idea.

"Couldn't we get Mr Jakes a proper card between us, and post it to him? We needn't sign it."

They all counted their pennies, and

then they went to look at Miss Muggins' greeting cards. The prettiest said, "To my Husband" – but Mr Jakes might think Mrs Jakes had sent it! Another (cheaper) said, "To my Friend". And they decided on that.

Billy Blunt wrote the name and address with his pen, and they bought a real stamp, and posted the card in the letter-box (though Mr Jakes lived only next door).

And then Milly-Molly-Mandy and little-friend-Susan ran home.

Well! – you can guess how pleased and surprised Mr Jakes the postman was to have to deliver such a nice card to himself! But, actually, it was Miss Crisp the postmistress who found Billy Blunt's little package. And she saw it was just a bit of nonsense, and threw it away!

4

Milly-Molly-Mandy
Goes Excavating

Once upon a time, as Milly-Molly-Mandy was going into school, she noticed a number of young men come striding along from the crossroads and up Hooker's Hill. They were carrying spades and pickaxes and things, but somehow they didn't look like men who were mending the roads.

"I wonder what they're going to do," said Milly-Molly-Mandy.

"They're going to do excavating," said Billy Blunt. "I heard my dad talking about it. They've got permission."

"What's excavating?"

"Digging up old things," said Billy Blunt.

"Like buried treasure? That sort of thing? How do they know where to do it?"

"They guess," said Billy Blunt. "They guess ancient Britons might have lived up there once. They just want to find out."

It sounded rather exciting. Milly-Molly-Mandy wished she could go digging instead of just going to school!

Next Saturday morning she took Toby the dog for a walk down to the village, rather hoping to hear more about the excavating. As she passed the corn-shop she saw Billy Blunt hanging over the side-gate.

"Hullo!" said Milly-Molly-Mandy. "What are you doing?"

Billy Blunt didn't answer. (Anyone could see he was doing nothing.) But after a moment he said:

"Want to see something?"

Of course Milly-Molly-Mandy said yes, at once.

And Billy Blunt drew his hand slowly out of his pocket and opened it. There was a

flat, round thing in it, streaked brown and green.

"What d'you make of that?" he asked.

"What is it? Is it money? Where did you find it?"

"I excavated it."

"You didn't! Where?"

"In our garden. By the bonfire heap. I was just digging a bit, to see if there might be anything – you never know – and I dug this up."

"It must be ancient!" said Milly-Molly-Mandy. "Have you shown it to anybody?"

"Not yet." Billy Blunt rubbed it carefully with his handkerchief. "Mother's busy, and Dad's got customers."

"Let's show it to Mr Rudge!" said Milly-

Molly-Mandy. "He knows about iron and such things; he'll know if it's valuable."

So they went along to the forge, where the blacksmith was blowing up his fire.

Milly-Molly-Mandy peeped in the doorway.

"Mr Rudge! Billy Blunt's excavated something!" she told him; "and we want to know if you think it's very valuable!"

The blacksmith looked round with a twinkle in his eye. He held out one great grimy hand, working the bellows with the other, and Billy Blunt put the precious coin into it.

Mr Rudge examined it one side, then the other. Then he rubbed it on his big leather apron and looked again.

"Hmmm," he said solemnly. "Georgian, I'd say. Yes. Undoubtedly."

"Is that very ancient?" asked Milly-Molly-Mandy.

"What's it worth?" asked Billy Blunt.

"If you're asking me, don't you take a ha'penny less than a penny for it. But mind you," he added, "if it's treasure-trove it may belong to the Crown." He gave the coin back and turned again to his fire. Billy Blunt

42

and Milly-Molly-Mandy came out into the sunshine, looking to see what all that rubbing had done.

"Looks like there's a head –" said Billy Blunt; "can't see any date."

"What's treasure-trove mean?" asked Milly-Molly-Mandy.

"Dunno. P'raps if you dig up treasure you aren't supposed to keep it."

Then Milly-Molly-Mandy had an idea.

"If you dug this out of your garden maybe there's some more there! Can't you go excavating again? I'll help."

So they went back to the Blunts' garden, beside the corn-shop, and Billy Blunt led the way round the rhubarb-bed to the end by the rubbish-heap and the bonfire.

"It's awfully hard under here ..."

He picked up a trowel and handed Milly-Molly-Mandy a rusty knife to dig with, and they began jabbing about in the earth and weeds. But there didn't seem to be anything else but stones. (Plenty of them.)

Presently Milly-Molly-Mandy said:

"It's awfully hard under here – feels like rock."

"Where?" said Billy Blunt. He came over and used his trowel. "Looks like cement—"

"Perhaps it's buried treasure cemented in!" said Milly-Molly-Mandy.

"Fetch a spade out of the shed there," ordered Billy Blunt. "Hurry!"

So Milly-Molly-Mandy ran and fetched him a spade, and she took over the trowel.

And they could see there *was* something, underneath the earth and weeds!

"It's got an iron lid!" panted Milly-Molly-Mandy.

"It's an iron chest, cemented down!" puffed Billy Blunt.

They got the top scraped clear. It was square and rusty, with a kind of loop to lift it by.

"This is buried treasure all right!"

Billy Blunt was red with excitement.

Milly-Molly-Mandy wanted to jump and shout, but she was too busy.

The lid was awfully heavy. They tried to lever it up, but they couldn't.

"You'll have to tell your father and mother, won't you?" said Milly-Molly-Mandy, at last.

Billy Blunt dropped the spade and dashed indoors. And presently Mr Blunt came out, in his apron, and walked over to their hole.

He took one look.

"*That?*" he said. "What-ever will you be up to next? That's only the cover of the drain!" When he could stop laughing he added, "Just as well you unearthed it, though – there might have been trouble if the authorities knew it had got covered over. Don't know how it happened—"

"But look, Dad. I found this –" Billy Blunt showed his piece of money. "We thought there might be some more. It's quite ancient, isn't it? The blacksmith said Georgian—"

Mr Blunt scraped with his pocket knife a moment. Then he fished a few coins from his trousers' pocket, picked out a penny and handed it over with the other. "There's your same Georgian coin," he chuckled, "King George V – only a bit cleaner. Yours looks as if it's been on the bonfire!"

Well! It was all very disappointing. But anyhow, those two pennies bought two fine peppermint humbugs from Miss Muggins' shop. And, sucking away together, Billy Blunt and Milly-Molly-

Mandy both agreed it had really been quite fun while it lasted.

But they hoped the excavators up on Hooker's Hill were having better luck!

5

Milly-Molly-Mandy
Has an Adventure

Once upon a time, one Saturday afternoon, Milly-Molly-Mandy had quite an adventure.

There was a special children's film showing at the cinema in the next village, and Milly-Molly-Mandy and little-friend-Susan were going to it, by bus, quite by themselves!

"Keep together, and don't talk to strangers," said Mother, giving Milly-Molly-Mandy the money for the cinema and for the bus, there and back.

"But supposing strangers speak to us?"

said Milly-Molly-Mandy.

"Always answer politely," said Mother, "but no more than that."

So Milly-Molly-Mandy set off from the nice white cottage with the thatched roof, down the road with the hedges each side to the Moggs' cottage where little-friend-Susan was waiting for her. And they walked on together to the cross-roads, feeling very important, to catch the bus.

There was plenty of time, but they thought they had better run the last part of the way, to be on the safe side. But nobody was waiting at the cross-roads, so they wondered if they had missed the bus after all.

Then one or two people came up and

waited, so it couldn't have gone. And presently it came in sight.

And just as everybody was getting on who do you suppose came along and got on too? – Why, Billy Blunt!

Milly-Molly-Mandy and little-friend-Susan took their seats and paid their half-fares, and pocketed the change carefully (three pennies for Milly-Molly-Mandy, a threepenny piece for little-friend-Susan). And then they sat looking out of the windows to make sure they didn't get carried past the cinema.

Billy Blunt had made for a seat right in front, looking as if he were quite used to doing this sort of thing by himself. (But he couldn't have been, really!) He managed to be first to get off the moment the bus stopped, so they didn't actually see if he went into the cinema.

Inside, it was so dark you couldn't recognize anybody. Milly-Molly-Mandy and little-friend-Susan held hands tight, not to lose one another.

It was all very exciting.

And so was the film. They wished it needn't end. When it was all over it seemed funny to come out into daylight again and find the same ordinary world outside.

They saw Billy Blunt coming away, talking with another boy. So they walked straight to the bus-stop and began waiting. (The bus ran every hour, and if one had just gone they might be a long time getting home.)

Suddenly little-friend-Susan said loudly, "My money!" and began rummaging in her coat-pocket.

Milly-Molly-Mandy said, "Why? Where?" and began rummaging in her own. (But her three pennies were safe all right.)

"My threepenny piece!" said little-friend-Susan; "I had it here . . ."

She looked in her right-hand pocket, then in her left, then in her hands. Then Milly-Molly-Mandy looked.

Then they looked on the pavement, and in the gutter.

"You must have dropped it in the cinema, Susan," said Milly-Molly-Mandy. "Let's go back and ask."

"But I didn't," said little-friend-Susan. "I felt it in my pocket as we came out."

So they looked all along the pavement. But still they couldn't find it.

"Well, we've just got to walk home," said Milly-Molly-Mandy, at last. "You can't go by yourself. We'll have to walk together."

"It's too far to walk," said little-friend-Susan, nearly crying.

Just then Billy Blunt came up to join the queue. Milly-Molly-Mandy said to him, "She's lost her money!"

Billy Blunt didn't know what to say, so he said nothing.

A gipsy woman standing near with a baby and big basket said, "There now! Lost your money, have you, ducks?"

Milly-Molly-Mandy said again, "We've got to walk home."

Billy Blunt said, "It's too far." Then he said, "Here, have mine. I'll manage."

But Milly-Molly-Mandy and little-friend-Susan said together, "You can't walk that far all by yourself!"

The gipsy woman began fumbling under her apron for her purse.

"I may have just a spare copper or two—" she said. "Where does the little lady live? I'll call on her ma, and she can

"SHE'S LOST HER MONEY!"

pay me back some day!"

Milly-Molly-Mandy, remembering what Mother had said, answered politely, "No, thank you very much!" – when at that moment the bus came in sight.

"Here!" said Billy Blunt, holding out his money.

Milly-Molly-Mandy and little-friend-Susan didn't like to take it. They couldn't think *what* to do.

An old truck laden with empty cans and things was coming rattling down the road. It overtook the bus and was just clattering past the bus-stop when Milly-Molly-Mandy suddenly started waving her arms wildly at it.

"Cyril, stop! Cyril!" she shouted.

The truck slowed down, and a tousled head looked back from the driver's seat.

"It's Cyril!" Milly-Molly-Mandy told the others, excitedly. "He drives things to the station for Uncle sometimes!" She ran forward. "Oh, Cyril! May I ride home with you?" she asked.

"You may not," said Cyril. "In that get-up? – I'd have your ma after me. Anyhow, I'm not going by your house today – only to the cross-roads."

Little-friend-Susan pulled at Milly-Molly-Mandy's sleeve.

"But, Milly-Molly-Mandy! You know we've got to keep together!"

The bus was drawing up. People were beginning to get on.

Billy Blunt asked Cyril quickly, "Can you take *me*?"

"If you want," said Cyril. "But hop on quick."

The bus was tooting for him to get out of the way.

Billy Blunt pushed his money at little-friend-Susan, saying, "Go on – hurry!" Then he clambered into the truck beside Cyril, helped by Cyril's very grubby hand, and off they went rattling down the road.

"Now then, you two!" the bus-driver called out of his small side-window, "are you coming with us or aren't you? We haven't got all day, you know."

And Milly-Molly-Mandy and little-friend-Susan (full of smiles) rushed to scramble on to the bus. And off they went, after the truck, down the road, and along the winding leafy lanes.

Billy Blunt was waiting at the cross-roads to see them arrive. He looked quite pleased with himself! (He had an oily smear down one leg, and his hands were black.)

"I got here quicker than you did," was all he said, when they thanked him.

And – do you know! – that threepenny piece of little-friend-Susan's was found, after all!

It had worked through a small hole in her coat-pocket down into the lining. And she was able to work it out again and pay Billy Blunt back the next day.

6

Milly-Molly-Mandy
on Bank Holiday

Once upon a time, one fine day, Milly-Molly-Mandy couldn't think what to do with herself.

It felt as if something specially nice should be done, as it was a Bank Holiday. But Father and Mother and Grandpa and Grandma and Uncle and Aunty all said they were busy, and everywhere would be so crowded today, and they preferred to stay at home.

"Why not go and play with little-friend-Susan?" said Mother, getting out jam-pots ready for jam-making.

"Get yourself some sweets, if the shop's open," said Father, feeling in his trousers' pocket.

So Milly-Molly-Mandy called to Toby the dog and wandered down the road with the hedges each side, to the Moggs' cottage.

Little-friend-Susan was outside, minding her baby sister.

They both had clean frocks and their hats on.

"Hullo, Milly-Molly-Mandy!" said little-friend-Susan. "It's Bank Holiday today. Father's going to take us all out on the red bus. I wish you were coming too!"

So did Milly-Molly-Mandy. But as she wasn't she called to Toby the dog and wandered on down to the village.

Miss Muggins' shop had its blind half-down over the toys and sweets in the window. But Milly-Molly-Mandy tried the handle, just in case, and Miss Muggins' Jilly peeped through the collarettes and gloves hanging across the glass of the door.

When she saw who was there Miss Muggins' Jilly stooped and said through the letter-box slit:

"We aren't open today, Milly-Molly-

Mandy. It's Bank Holiday. My aunty's taking me to my granny's, by the red bus."

(Toby the dog was so surprised at a voice coming from the letter-box that he barked and barked!)

But next moment the door was unlocked, and Miss Muggins' Jilly (in her best white hat) stepped outside, followed by Miss Muggins herself (in her best black).

As she locked the door behind her and put the key in her bag Miss Muggins said:

"Good morning, Milly-Molly-Mandy. Now we mustn't delay, or we shall miss the bus."

And Milly-Molly-Mandy, holding Toby the dog, watched them go hurrying down to the cross-roads, where several people were standing waiting.

The red bus arrived just as Mr Moggs, carrying the baby, and Mrs Moggs, with little-friend-Susan, came running and waving by the short-cut across the fields, only *just* in time. Everybody scrambled aboard; the bus gave a "ping!" and off they all went, away into the distance.

And you wouldn't believe how empty the village felt!

There was only Mr Smale the grocer (in his shirtsleeves) reading a newspaper at his doorway, and Milly-Molly-Mandy standing with Toby the dog, wondering what to do next.

There didn't seem to be anything.

Then, round the corner by the forge, who

should come along but Billy Blunt, carrying an old rusty tea-tray under his arm!

"Hullo!" he said, grinning.

"Hullo!" said Milly-Molly-Mandy, rather dolefully. "It's Bank Holiday today."

"I know," said Billy Blunt. "And I mean to have one. You can come along if you want."

"Where to?" asked Milly-Molly-Mandy. "What are you going to do? What's that thing?"

"It's a tea-tray," said Billy Blunt. "I found it on Mr Rudge's junk-heap. I shall put it back when I've done. Come on if you're coming."

So, feeling very curious, Milly-Molly-Mandy and Toby the dog followed him.

They walked to the cross-roads, then up

"HULLO!" HE SAID, GRINNING

the steep hilly road beyond. Presently they climbed a low fence and through a lot of brambles and things, till they came out on a high meadow looking down on the village.

"Here's the place," said Billy Blunt.

And he solemnly placed his tray on the ground and sat on it. And with a few shoves and pushes he went sliding down over the grass, faster and faster down the bank, leaving Milly-Molly-Mandy and Toby the dog shouting and barking behind him, till at last he came to a stop by the hedge at the bottom of the meadow.

"How's that?" he said triumphantly, as he climbed panting back to the top again, dragging the tray. "Want a go? You have to mind out for the nettles by the hedge . . ."

So Milly-Molly-Mandy sat on the tray, and Billy Blunt gave her a good shove. And off she went down the bank, with the wind in her hair and Toby the dog racing alongside, till she spilled over in the long grass just short of the nettles.

Then Billy Blunt took several more turns till he was quite out of breath, and Milly-Molly-Mandy had another go.

They only stopped at last because it began to feel like dinner-time. They were very hungry and very warm (and rather grubby too!).

"Well!" said Milly-Molly-Mandy, as they started homeward, "this is a proper Bank Holiday, isn't it?"

"Well –" said Billy Blunt, "I think Bank Holidays are meant so that people in banks can stop counting up their money. It's not this sort of bank really, you know."

"This is the sort of Bank Holiday I like best, anyhow," said Milly-Molly-Mandy.

7

Milly-Molly-Mandy Has American Visitors

Once upon a time Milly-Molly-Mandy felt rather excited.

Aunty had a letter with a foreign stamp on from her brother Tom, saying that he

and his wife and children were coming over from America to visit their English relatives.

Aunty had not seen her brother Tom since he was quite young, and had never seen his wife, or their children, though they and Milly-Molly-Mandy had exchanged letters and paper dolls.

"Will Sallie and Lallie and Buddy come to stay here?" asked Milly-Molly-Mandy. "Where will they sleep?"

"We must think," said Mother. "Your Uncle Tom and Aunty Sadie will have the spare room, of course, and Sallie and Lallie might squeeze together in your little room. Perhaps we can make up a bed on the floor for Buddy beside his parents."

"But where will I sleep?" asked Milly-Molly-Mandy.

"You'll have to have a little floor-bed too, beside Father and me," said Mother.

Milly-Molly-Mandy thought that sounded rather fun. (Certainly nicer than wandering around all night with nowhere to sleep!)

"It won't be for long," said Aunty, folding up her letter; "there are other relatives to visit."

Then everybody in the nice white cottage with the thatched roof got very busy. Father picked some of his best fruit and vegetables; Mother made lots of pies and cakes; and Grandpa groomed Twinkletoes and washed the pony-trap; Grandma crocheted a fine new tea-cosy;

Uncle collected plenty of eggs from his chickens; Aunty cleaned and polished all the rooms; and Milly-Molly-Mandy helped where she could, and was very useful indeed.

When she told Billy Blunt about it, he grinned and said:

"You'll have to learn to talk American, now!" (Which set Milly-Molly-Mandy wondering, until she remembered how she and Sallie and Lallie and Buddy had written to each other in English!)

Well, the important day came.

Uncle and Aunty went by bus to the railway station, to meet the train. And Grandpa, with Milly-Molly-Mandy and Twinkletoes and the pony-trap, went to meet the bus at the cross-roads as it returned, to drive Sallie and Lallie and Buddy and their mother and the luggage home.

There wasn't room in the pony-trap for everybody. So Uncle and Aunty and Milly-Molly-Mandy all walked home together with Uncle Tom, through the village and along the road with hedges each side.

Uncle Tom looked round about him, saying "Well, this sure is a bit of the old country!" as they went.

When Milly-Molly-Mandy showed him the corn-shop where Billy Blunt lived, and the Moggs' cottage where little-friend-Susan lived, Uncle Tom said, "You don't say!" (though she had just said it!).

When they came to the nice white cottage with the thatched roof Uncle Tom said, "Well, this sure looks a picture!" (though it just looked like home to Milly-Molly-Mandy).

The new Aunty Sadie was helping Mother and Grandma and Aunty in the kitchen, when they got in, and Sallie and Lallie and Buddy were running about, all chattering together, and it all sounded very exciting!

The grown-ups sat down at the big table, and the young ones had a small table to themselves (there wasn't room for everybody otherwise).

They talked about the big boat they had come over on, and about the big place they had come from (which was America, of course), and Uncle Tom told stories of Indians and horse-riding and deserts, and it was all terribly exciting!

They didn't a bit want to go to bed at bedtime.

But that was exciting too, going to bed in new places – Sallie and Lallie in Milly-Molly-Mandy's little attic room, Buddy in a makeshift bed in the spare room, and Milly-Molly-Mandy herself on a mattress on the floor in Father's and Mother's room.

She lay listening to the grown-ups' talk rumbling on and on downstairs, until at last she fell asleep, and it was morning again.

After breakfast they went out to play in

the yard, and Milly-Molly-Mandy showed her cousins the old tumbledown pigsty. (It was quite clean and empty, no pigs lived in it now.)

"This is my house," said Milly-Molly-Mandy, "but you can come inside. We must shut the gate, to keep the lions out."

"You don't have lions," said Buddy.

"Oh, we do!" said Milly-Molly-Mandy. "There's one now! Quick! Hurry! Hurry!"

And they all rushed squealing into the pigsty, as Toby the dog came capering up to see what was going on. Milly-Molly-Mandy held the broken gate shut.

"We can't come out till he goes away," she said; "he might eat us!"

Presently Toby the dog went off to see

what was moving round by the shed, and they all crept out to gather up a few windfall apples so that they wouldn't starve!

They were just hurrying back with them to the sty, when they heard a frightful hooting noise. And a strange figure came leaping towards them.

(It was Billy Blunt with an old sack over one shoulder and a chicken's tail-

THEY ALL RUSHED SCREAMING BACK INTO THE STY

feather stuck in his hair!)

"It's Indians! Run! Run!" shrieked Milly-Molly-Mandy.

And they all rushed screaming back into the sty and pushed the gate to, only *just* in time!

"You know, I think he may be quite a kind Indian, really," said Milly-Molly-Mandy, then. "Would you like an apple?" And she held out a nice one over the gate.

"Wah!" said Billy Blunt, taking and biting it.

So they let him come in. And they all huddled together in the pigsty, eating windfall apples (to keep themselves from starving), and throwing the cores for the "lion" to run after outside.

Sallie and Lallie and Buddy thought England was quite an exciting sort of place! They would have liked to stay much longer at the nice white cottage with the thatched roof, but there were other things they had to see.

When the day came for them to leave Uncle Tom gave Milly-Molly-Mandy a real dollar bill – to use

when she came to visit America one day, he said. Milly-Molly-Mandy is keeping it safe in her treasure-box.

8

Milly-Molly-Mandy and a Wet Day

Once upon a time, one morning, when Milly-Molly-Mandy went off to school, it was raining and raining. (But she had on her rubber boots and raincoat and hood.)

When she got to the Moggs' cottage there was little-friend-Susan (in rubber boots and raincoat and hood)

watching for her at the door.

"Oh, what a nasty wet, rainy day!" said little-friend-Susan, running out to join her.

"Mother says, if we keep going it won't hurt," said Milly-Molly-Mandy.

So they kept going, trudging along together down the wet road with the wet hedges each side, very glad to have each other to squeal to when the cold raindrops dripped off their noses.

When they got to the duck-pond all the little ducks were flapping and quacking away as if quite enjoying such a nice wet, rainy day! When they got to the village Billy Blunt (in thick shoes and raincoat) was dashing from the corn-shop; and Miss Muggins' niece Jilly (in new red rubber boots and her mackintosh over her head) was running from the draper's shop. They hadn't far to go, of course, but Milly-Molly-Mandy and little-friend-Susan arrived at school almost the same time, together with some other boys and girls who came by the red bus to the cross-roads.

They all hung up their coats and hats and changed their shoes, flapping and quacking away together like a lot of little ducks, as if they too quite enjoyed the rainy day! (Milly-Molly-Mandy and little-friend-Susan were dry and warm as toast after their long walk.)

When morning school was over the rain had stopped for a bit. But everywhere was still sopping wet, and in the road outside the school gate was a great muddy puddle.

Milly-Molly-Mandy, and a few others who went home for dinner (some who lived a long way off ate theirs at school), rather enjoyed having to wade through. Billy Blunt chose the deepest place. But Miss Muggins' Jilly, who tried to jump over, made a fine splash.

"It's a good thing we've got our mackintoshes on!" said Milly-Molly-Mandy.

"We ought to be ducks!" said little-friend-Susan.

"Road ought to be mended," said Billy Blunt.

He looked around and picked up some stones which he threw into the puddle. Milly-Molly-Mandy threw in a few bits

Miss Muggins' Jilly . . . tried to jump over

of broken slate, and little-friend-Susan a handful of leaves and twigs. But it didn't make much difference.

"You'll get yourselves muddy," said Miss Muggins' Jilly.

"We need more stuff," said Billy Blunt.

So they looked about in hedges and ditches, picking up anything to throw in.

"Put 'em just here," said Billy Blunt. "No sense throwing them all over the place."

"I think I'd better go in now," said Miss Muggins' Jilly. "My aunty wouldn't like me to get my new rubber boots wet."

"I thought that's what rubber boots were for," said Milly-Molly-Mandy.

"They're wet already, anyhow," said little-friend-Susan.

"Don't stand there jabbering," said Billy Blunt. "Get busy, or get out of the way."

So Miss Muggins' Jilly went off home. But Milly-Molly-Mandy and little-friend-Susan and Billy Blunt carried on, looking for things to throw into the puddle.

They found some nice bits of brick on the waste ground by the cross-roads. Also a splendid lump of broken paving-stone; but it was too heavy to carry, and they had to leave it after a struggle.

Then they had to hurry home to their dinners, and Milly-Molly-Mandy (with farthest to go) only *just* wasn't late for hers.

As soon as she could she hurried back to school, little-friend-Susan joining her on the way. But Billy Blunt was there already, adding fresh stones to mend the roadway. He had his box-on-wheels beside him.

"I got an idea while I was eating my pudding," said Billy Blunt. "We ought to be able to fetch that bit of paving-stone in this!"

So, with the little cart rattling and bumping along between them, they ran across the waste ground by the cross-roads.

And together they heaved and they pushed and they grunted, till they got the stone out of the long grass, on to the little cart.

And then they pulled and they pushed, and they grunted, till they got it wheeled over the rough ground into the roadway.

And then they heaved and they grunted

(which always seems to help!) till they slid the stone out into the middle of the puddle, with a fine muddy *splosh!*

"That's done it!" said Billy Blunt with satisfaction, wiping himself with some grass.

And then the bell rang, and they had to scurry in and tidy up.

When school was over everyone used the stepping-stones as they left, and kept dry and clean.

Then – what do you think? – as the bus that took some of the children home stopped for them at the cross-roads a grey-haired lady got off, and came down to the school gate.

She asked Milly-Molly-Mandy, who was standing nearest:

"Has Miss Edwards come out yet? Would you mind telling her her mother's here?"

Milly-Molly-Mandy was surprised. (She had never thought of Teacher as having a mother!) Miss Edwards came hurrying out, very pleased, to welcome the visitor and take her into her own cottage next door.

And they both used the stepping-stones and were glad to find the road had been so nicely mended — because Mrs Edwards hadn't any rubber boots on, only lady's shoes and an umbrella.

"Well, now!" said Mother, when Milly-Molly-Mandy came running home to the nice white cottage with the thatched roof. "What have you been up to? Have you got wet?"

"No!" said Milly-Molly-Mandy. "We kept going, like you said, and I'm warm as anything!"

9

Milly-Molly-Mandy Makes some Toffee

Once upon a time Milly-Molly-Mandy with little-friend-Susan and Billy Blunt were in the village,

planning
how to
spend
their
pennies
to get
the most
sweets.
Miss

Muggins' shop had the usual jars of raspberry-drops and aniseed balls; Mr Smale the grocer's had coconut ice and caramels.

"But they go so quickly," said Milly-Molly-Mandy.

"And they're expensive," said little-friend-Susan.

"Sugar's cheaper," said Billy Blunt, his nose to the glass, "but not so interesting."

"Mother makes toffee sometimes, with sugar," said Milly-Molly-Mandy. "I wonder if we could!"

"How does your mother make it?" asked little-friend-Susan.

"She puts sugar, and butter, and some vinegar, in a frying-pan, and boils it up," said Milly-Molly-Mandy.

"Vinegar!" said Billy Blunt. "Can't be nice."

"It is then!" said Milly-Molly-Mandy. "It's lovely!"

"Well, why don't we buy sugar, and ask if we can make some ourselves?" said little-friend-Susan.

"If you think you know how –" said Billy Blunt. "Don't want to waste things."

So they all went into the shop and put their pennies on the counter, and Mr Smale the grocer weighed out sugar and handed it over. And they ran all the way to the nice white cottage with the thatched roof (where Milly-Molly-Mandy lived), into the kitchen where Mother was busy cooking.

"Mother!" said Milly-Molly-Mandy; "may we make toffee all by ourselves? We've bought some sugar."

"Yes," said Billy Blunt.

"Please," said little-friend-Susan.

Mother said: "Very well. You may use the stove after dinner, directly the washing-up is done, and I won't watch you!"

So, soon after dinner, Billy Blunt and little-friend-Susan came running round again.

Milly-Molly-Mandy was all ready for them. Mother was at her sewing-machine, but she only glanced up to say hullo.

"You won't take any notice of us, will you, Mother?" said Milly-Molly-Mandy.

"No! I'm too busy," said Mother.

So they set to work.

They tipped their sugar into the frying-pan, with a knob of butter and a spoonful of water to start it melting. Milly-Molly-Mandy stirred with a wooden spoon, little-friend-Susan found a dish for the toffee, and Billy Blunt greased it well.

"You don't really put vinegar in it, do you?" he said.

"You do, don't you, Mother?" said Milly-Molly-Mandy.

The sewing-machine stopped a moment. "I usually add a small spoonful, to lessen the sweet-ness," said Mother. "There's some in the larder." And the machine rattled on again.

So Billy Blunt fetched the bottle, and they measured a spoonful into the pan.

"We have to try some in cold water to see when it's done," said Milly-Molly-Mandy. (She always liked that part!)

So little-friend-Susan fetched a cupful, and they dripped a few drops in off the spoon. But it only made the water look dirty.

"It goes in hard balls when it's done," said Milly-Molly-Mandy.

"Then it isn't done," said Billy Blunt.

"It hasn't boiled properly," said little-friend-Susan.

Presently Mother said:

"There's rather an odd smell, isn't there?"

"You promised not to watch us!" said Milly-Molly-Mandy.

"I'm not watching," said Mother, "but I can't help smelling."

THEY MEASURED A SPOONFUL INTO THE PAN

"It's the vinegar,"
said Billy Blunt.

"P'raps it's
getting done," said
little-friend-Susan.

So they tried
a bit more in cold
water. It tasted odd, but not done.

Presently Father came in from working
in his vegetable garden.

"Hullo? What's going on here?" he asked,
sniffing.

"We're making toffee!" said Milly-Molly-
Mandy.

"All by ourselves!" said little-friend-Susan.

"We bought our own sugar," said Billy
Blunt.

"What's the flavouring?" asked Father. "Onion?" He got his seed labels from the mantelshelf and went out again.

They all laughed. Fancy onion in toffee! All the same – "It does smell sort of funny," said Milly-Molly-Mandy.

"P'raps the pan was oniony?" said little-friend-Susan.

"No!" said Mother, over her shoulder.

"It's that vinegar," said Billy Blunt again.

Suddenly Mother asked:

"Do you always read labels carefully when you cook? It's one of the first rules."

"I read that bottle," said Billy Blunt. "It said vinegar." And he brought the bottle to show her.

The label read – *Garlic Vinegar!*

"Ohhh!" exclaimed Milly-Molly-Mandy and little-friend-Susan, loudly.

Mother dropped her sewing.

"I should have remembered there were two sorts of vinegar in the larder," she said, "but I so seldom use that smaller bottle. I wonder if you can cover up with some other flavour, peppermint perhaps?"

She found a tiny bottle in the cupboard.

So (reading the label with great care) they added a few drops of peppermint essence to the toffee, before turning it out into the greased dish to cool before cutting it up.

The rest of the afternoon, they played down by the stream, with Toby the dog. And, do you know, they all thought the toffee wasn't really so bad! (Father said he had never tasted better garlic-toffee!) And it certainly lasted them a long while.

But I don't fancy they will make any more like it – they read labels very carefully now!

About the Author

Joyce Lankester Brisley was born over a hundred years ago, on 6 February 1896. She had two sisters: an elder one, Ethel, and Nina, who was just a year younger than Joyce. The family lived in Bexhill-on-Sea in Sussex, in a house so close to the sea that when there was a very high tide the waves would come right into the garden. Joyce's father ran a chemist's shop in the town. Her mother enjoyed drawing and painting, but had to spend most of her time looking after the home and her children.

Joyce and her sisters were all good at art, like their mother, and went to evening classes at Hastings School of Art, taking the train there and back along the coast. By the time they were teenagers, "Eth" (as Ethel was always known in the family) was having her pictures accepted for exhibitions at the Royal Academy in London and was soon selling paintings as a result. Then, through a friend, the girls were invited to meet Miss Brown of the magazine *Home Chat.* They quickly began to do illustrations for this magazine, so for the first time all three sisters started to earn money for themselves.

This money was soon to become very important for the family. In 1912, when Joyce was sixteen, her parents separated. In her diary (writing in French as if to keep it a secret) she recorded that her father wanted his family to leave the house. They stayed until Joyce and

Nina had finished their term at art school, then the three girls moved with their mother to South London, where Eth had found them a tiny flat.

In London, Joyce and Nina enrolled at the Lambeth School of Art in 1912 – an uncle kindly agreed to pay the fees for both girls. They studied there five days a week for two years. In 1913 they moved to a house with a large room that the three girls could use as a studio.

The outbreak of the First World War in 1914 meant that food was scarce. Their mother had to spend a lot of time searching for meat and vegetables she could afford, while the girls worked hard earning money from illustrations for magazines, newspapers and advertisements. Joyce writes in her diary about drawing advertisements for Cherry Blossom boot polish and Mansion floor polish. She also writes about the German bombing raids on London – describing how, in September 1916, the sisters had to get up in the middle of the night and go downstairs for safety, still in their nightclothes and bedtime plaits.

Despite the war and constant worries about money, family life continued happily throughout this time. In 1917 Joyce records in her diary that Nina (daringly) wanted to cut her hair short, and Eth longed to do the same, but Joyce felt "I couldn't – it wouldn't suit me well at all". The sisters obviously got along very well together, but nevertheless Joyce wished she had some privacy. She was delighted when, shortly after her twenty-first birthday, she was able to have a room of her own – "My longing, for years and years."

In 1918 they all moved again, to a house with

a larger studio. Joyce went with her mother and sisters to the local Christian Science Church. There they met an artist who worked for *The Christian Science Monitor*. As a result, both Joyce and Nina began submitting stories and drawings to the paper, and it was on the Children's Page in October 1925 that the first story about Milly-Molly-Mandy appeared. The idea had come into Joyce's mind one day when "the sun was shining and I longed to be out in the country instead of sitting indoors all day, earning a living . . ."

Milly-Molly-Mandy was an immediate success and soon began to gain a strong following among readers. Joyce records that:

"*. . . boys and girls began writing letters to the paper, to the editors and to Milly-Molly-Mandy herself, wanting to know more about her, asking,*

Could she come for a holiday by the sea? Could she have a baby sister to take out riding in the pram? (She couldn't, as she was an 'only' child, but little-friend-Susan could, and did.) Some of the letters enclosed foreign stamps for Billy Blunt's collection (so generous!). One boy wrote all the way from Australia to tell me that 'Father' was shown digging with his wrong foot on the spade (for it seems the left foot is the right foot for digging with!). I wrote back to thank him and promised to alter the drawing before it went into a book – as you may see I did, for it's nice to get things quite correct."

Joyce went on writing stories about Milly-Molly-Mandy for the rest of her life, but she wrote about other characters too, in books such as *Marigold in Godmother's House* (1934) and *Adventures of Purl and Plain* (1941). She also illustrated stories by other authors and was specially chosen by her publisher, George Harrap, to draw the pictures for the first edition of Ursula Moray Williams's *Adventures of the Little Wooden Horse* (1938).

Joyce always remained close to her sisters. Nina, who became the first and much-loved illustrator of the Chalet School stories by Elinor M. Brent-Dyer, was the only one to marry. Ethel died in 1961, and Nina and Joyce died within a few months of each other, in 1978.

Joyce Lankester Brisley seems to have been rather a shy person and she obviously didn't like publicity. Once, after two of her pictures had been accepted by the Royal Academy and a journalist wanted to interview her, she telegraphed at once that she "would be out". Maybe she was a bit like Milly-Molly-Mandy herself – happy to be busily getting on with whatever task or errand she'd set herself for the day, and content with whatever good fortune life might bring her.

Collect them all!

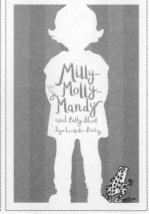